Idiots' Books

Idiots'Books
100 South Queen Street
Chestertown, MD 21620

ISBN 978-1-61658-895-3
Copyright © 2010

From the Inside Out

By Matthew Swanson
Illustrated by Robbi Behr

*For our editors,
our second chances*

My life collides with Vanessa's life at a meeting for alcoholics who don't believe in God. I walk through the door and there she is, a lighthouse in a sea of sad gray faces. As I put on my name tag and notice the name on hers, my life cleaves neatly into future and past.

I found the flyer for the workshop taped to the subway wall. There among the clutter and congestion was a message that intrigued me: Unable to appeal to a higher power, we will immerse ourselves in craft and work together to discover new ways of sating our thirsts. We will aim to rebuild from the inside out.

We start in a circle that first night, each of us giving his name and story. There are 13 men and 8 women. I choose the chair directly across from Vanessa's so that it will not seem out of place to stare. She is there at the urging of her parole officer. Attending the workshop is an alternative to community service and also reduces her fines. I am there to find a reason to continue with my life.

The meetings are each Monday, Wednesday, and Friday evening from seven to ten, scheduled to coincide with the most difficult hours. I leave work at six and eat my sandwich on the long train ride to the quiet clinic in the suburbs. I change trains twice on the way home. By the time I reach my building it is nearly eleven. I have taken to climbing the 23 flights to exhaust myself enough to fall asleep.

I have had to find a new home for the stemware, which used to greet me when I walked in the door, a loving family on exposed shelving. I have taken to dropping the glasses—a gift from an ex-girlfriend—from my kitchen window on nights when I need to hear something break.

I have placed liter bottles of sparkling water in the felt-lined cradles of my wine cabinet and purchased a closet safe in which to sequester the cabernet I had been saving to commemorate the birth of my first child. I turned the dial without looking at the numbers and mailed the combination in a letter to Aunt Elsa, who saves everything I send her in a shoebox. It is possible for me to open the safe some day, but it will be too difficult to manage in an evening's meltdown.

My life right now is about erecting sturdy barriers.

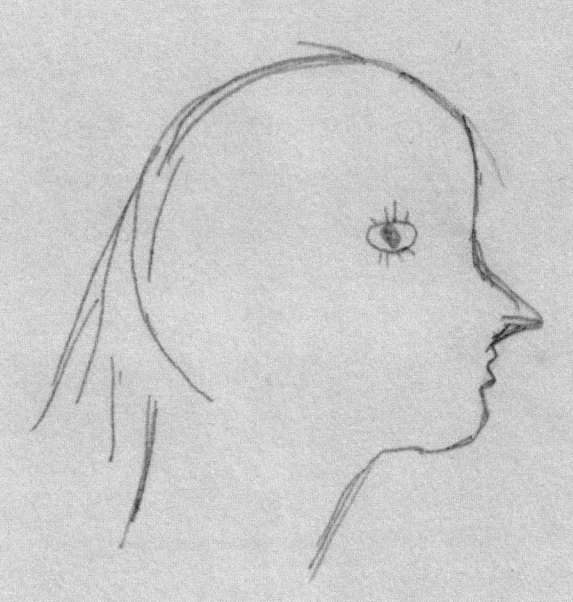

The director of the workshop is a nervous man with a broad, bald head. He wears thin glasses and a white lab coat as if to look the part of doctor—which, he has already assured us, he is not. We are to understand that his methods are based neither on medical evidence nor clinical trials. He simply feels that his is a good idea that should work if we will commit ourselves to it.

The director is a believer in art as a conduit to buried pain. He has set up stations with the materials needed for exploring various media and circulates throughout the evening, affirming our efforts. The old urges must find new channels to satisfaction, he tells us, and so we are encouraged to experiment. He does not judge or moralize. If boundaries are blurred now in these early, desperate moments, there will be time to rein us in later, once we have reestablished a base.

I have never been a creative man, but tonight I try my hand at charcoal. I ask the director for advice, but he admits that he knows nothing about technique. "Follow your hand," he tells me. "It doesn't matter what it looks like in the end."

Vanessa is posing for Charles as he sculpts her form in soft clay. She holds a sword aloft, sets her mouth in a scowl, and places her foot on a theater skull. I set up

my easel and begin to sketch. My efforts are unequal to her form, but I shrug off the impulse to self-censorship. Slowly, with effort, her figure emerges. Others might not know her from the scattered timber of my line, but I see her there, a private portrait only I can appreciate.

~

On Tuesdays and Thursdays, I get home from work so desperate for a drink that I have actually begun to jog. Years of fat have settled beneath my skin, and the effort of moving my bulk along the rooftop track creates a rare good feeling that feels the opposite of drunkeness.

I am so hungry for distraction on weekends that I have started watching football, learning the rules and regulations, substituting its patterns and rhythms for those I have abandoned. I don't understand a thing except the movement of the ball. There is a pleasing rush of sensation when my team wins and an unsettling agitation when it doesn't—both of which stand in for things that I remember and have missed.

I am glad to live alone so that no one can bear witness to my pain, though in a fantasy, there is someone to support me who does not judge or tire of my dark moods. I imagine Vanessa in the window seat, smoking a cigarette and reading a thin novel. The lights are dim

and I have just returned from work. We share veal and endive and crystal flutes of cool seltzer. From opposite ends of the long table we admire one another.

Some nights I have dreams of purging. All the wine I have ever drunk gushes forth in a solid red river. My mouth is a faucet; my throat is stiff with pressure from below, a sewer running in reverse. I am ruining a landscape of clean white tablecloths that goes on for miles.

~

Trudy and I are mixing water and flour for papier-mâché. We are making a piñata for the children who are coming to our open house the following week to visit with their sober parents for the first time. Phyllis is making construction paper cutouts to hang on the walls. We want the place to look cheerful and healthy when they arrive.

Vanessa is walking from group to group, offering her critique of the decorations. She tells me the piñata should be sturdy so that the children will have to work to get at the candy.

I have known since the opening mixer that Vanessa and I are bound to one another, two points in compatible orbit, destined for eventual, if far-off collision. Her desire is unspoken, though no less pronounced. Mine is impossible to mute.

am the most prolific artist of the group, though perhaps the least accomplished. The director praises my effort. My work hangs with that of the others, by clothespins on the wall of the meeting room. So far I have rendered Vanessa in watercolor, charcoal, mosaic, and gouache.

~

My parents call at intervals and leave their newsy messages. To anyone else their voices might seem warm and concerned, but I have become an expert in discerning the sounds of drunken patter.

People call. I do not answer. There is always an implied invitation to drink, a hook submerged in the meat of the worm.

For Marco, who has never taken me seriously, this latest stunt is the biggest laugh of all. Once he realizes I mean to stay sober, he makes it his mission to derail me.

~

The machine is extraordinary. It reminds me of the freshly detailed engine of a rocket. I am no match for the chromed tangle of pipes, nozzles, switches, and knobs, but Irwin takes to learning the nuances and proves born to play barista. The first night it is café Americano, but by Friday he has discovered the frothing

nozzle and we enjoy au lait all around. Irwin proceeds to take the coffee drink to new heights. Each night he arrives with new items: obscure extracts, imported powdered chocolates, the milk from a llama—known for producing exquisite foam.

His drinks are delicious, but the caffeine compounds my unease. No amount of exertion can will me to sleep, and I find myself having to give up yet another thing I can actually feel.

Irwin's fledgling sense of worth is tied to our enjoyment of his creations. I take a mock swig, coating my upper lip in a smile of cinnamon froth before sneaking to the lobby to dump the contents among the roots of the potted palm.

Vanessa shows less tact. She refuses the coffee to flaunt her strength. She orders an espresso and throws it in Irwin's face. She apologizes, then pouts, and then luxuriates in Irwin's insistence that the fault was all his.

~

After workshop one night, I wait for Vanessa on the bench outside the door. I want to give her a gift—her likeness done in pen and ink. When eventually she emerges, dangling on Eddie's arm, I find that I am mute.

Eddie, beaming, wishes me good night and praises my most recent watercolor. I thank him and comment that his macramé has been improving. Eddie demurs, noting that, with talent like mine, the sky is the limit.

While Eddie and I exchange affirmation, Vanessa examines my shoes. She taps her fingers on her hips, red nails flashing in the lamplight. She coughs to signal her impatience, and Eddie wishes me good night.

I watch as they walk to Eddie's car. As he opens her door, Vanessa turns her head and meets my gaze for a long moment. She doesn't wink or fawn, but her meaning is clear: Eddie is a float in a minor parade. Bide your time.

~

Marco is waiting outside my building when I get off the train. He is grinning and drunk, hot to go out and ruin things.

"Hello then," he says, "I've missed you, buddy."

He sways like a top at the end of its momentum. He is pickled in bourbon. I try to step around him, but he blocks my way. I don't want to touch him or even look at him. I will turn to dust.

He produces a bottle from his coat, offering. He takes a long, sexual pull.

Marco has never been a good person, but I've always enjoyed him when we're drunk. He plays my dark shadow, dragging me down alleyways, past limits, beyond myself to shame and exultation.

My mouth is idle and desperate and dry.

I step around Marco and into the lobby. He grabs my shirt, trying to follow. Clark the doorman is there. I have always tipped him well. He reads my look and acts decisively.

When Clark hits him, Marco doubles. He drops his bottle and bourbon hisses on the pavement. I want to fall on the puddle, letting it soak into my clothes, cutting my tongue on the glass, mixing my blood with the sidewalk grit.

Instead I thank Clark as Marco staggers away. Clark grins. He wishes this sort of thing happened more often.

~

After Eddie there is Benjamin, then Michael, then Irwin. I learn as weeks pass that part of Vanessa's strategy for winning my heart is proving to me first that she can have anything or anyone else she desires. I am sickened with jealousy, but the pain gives me grist; my crusade to stay sober has long since been eclipsed by my need to possess her.

It is ironic that in my darkest hour I have found the thing that might have saved me all along. The perfection of Vanessa—the many contradictions of her manner and bearing, the exquisite precision of her studied neglect—has given me strength to withstand the current torment. I must see her three times each week, from seven to ten; she is the brute momentum without which I would tumble from the sky.

~

The other women are thin blond wisps, ragweed wilting in Vanessa's long shadow. Trudy invites me for coffee in the playroom, and I join her to be kind. She wants to talk about the nostalgia she's been feeling for martinis, which were, to her, an uncomplicated friend who loved without condition. I allow that my cabernet was always there for me, though we did sometimes quarrel toward the end of an evening.

Trudy has poured her heart into learning the trumpet and asks if I'll listen. She has only been at it four weeks but is remarkably accomplished, considering. She admits that she no longer sleeps, that she has taken leave from work, that all she does is practice when she's not at workshop. She is preparing a piece for the talent show, she tells me.

ASK AMY

...I don't want to lose this person as a friend, but I find it bizarre that a woman in her 50s passes on this type of thing to both male and female friends.

She has been a loyal and good friend over the years. I would appreciate your advice.

— Confused

I'll take your word for it that this person is a good and loyal friend, but true friends don't persist in sending porn to other friends and then belittle them when they object.

Because you two have a long history together and you seem to value her friendship, you could give her another opportunity to respect your very reasonable boundary about receiving obscene material.

If she continues to send pornography to you, you should assume that your friendship has changed. Don't respond again and in fact burn her bridges if she chooses to.

Dear Amy: Our boss's mother died recently. Several staff members asked her about the funeral arrangements, and she told them she did not know. Later, she was telling one staff member about receiving a call and contacting a relative.

No one at our office attended the arrangements, but enough of us known to know that it was not a close family observance.

I represent the staff in an uncontested nomination of the time.

Some people want to take up a collection to buy the boss a gift in memory of her mother. Many in our office do not wish to contribute, feeling that since they were not informed of the arrangements it is obvious that the boss does not like or respect them. What is the right thing to do?

— Confused Co-Worker

The right thing to do is to express your sympathy for this loss.

You seem to view this as a social event to which you have not been invited. Funerals and memorial services are not birthday parties or baby showers and your reaction to this is petty.

It is obvious that you and others don't like or respect your boss, but all the same, her loss is not the appropriate venue for you to punish her for being unprofessional. This is a personal event and your response should be personal.

A small donation to a related charity or a remembrance gift would be thoughtful, but not at all necessary. An expression of sympathy through a card from you and your colleagues would be a kindness and doesn't demand that you all live together.

Dear Amy: I am a student and my professor gave a female student who is pregnant. At first she was hiding it, but now she's wearing maternity clothes, and it's very obvious. However, it's really starting to frustrate me that no one talks about the fact that she is pregnant except behind her back. The white elephant in the room, so to speak, is that she looks months along. Any ideas?

— Want to Say Congrats

Any woman starts to feel like public property late in her pregnancy, but your professor's pregnancy truly is none of your business, any more than it would be if she and her husband were going through the process of adopting a child or if she were a male professor whose wife was pregnant.

Relative to your profession, the white elephant in the room is regrettable.

If you can't concentrate on your studies because of your professor's condition, approach her after class. Ask her all the questions you want to ask. She will handle your query the best way she knows how and then most likely write me a letter expressing her frustration.

Dear Amy: I'm responding to letters in your column about people having baby showers for unwed mothers. I think baby showers are a shameless plea for stuff. I'm not at all convinced that is obligated. Even as a family member to participate in this shameless plug.

If you want to help find their attending such an endorsement of celebrating, it's perfectly reasonable to stay home from the shower.

The mail about this has been leveling. With the exception of men who have all seem to agree with unwed mothers should be warded with a baby shower are split on this issue because they have been to baby showers and they are celebrations not necessarily a reflection of marital status of the mother.

Write to Amy Dickinson at askamy@tribune.com or Amy, Chicago Tribune, 435 N. Michigan Ave., Chicago, Ill. 60611.

© 2009 by the Chicago Tribune. Distributed by Tribune Media Service.

CELEBRATIONS
ENGAGEMENTS, WEDDINGS, ANNIVERSARIES AND SPECIAL EVENTS

Talbert
Diamond Anniversary
Congratulations to Edward James and Jane Mae... who were married on April... 1949 in Washington, D.C. at the home of Jane's aunt and uncle,

60th Anniversary
Ralph John and Margaret (McDowell) Wydro of Bethesda, Maryland were married on April 8, 1939 at Columbia Heights, Washington, D.C. John is a World War II veteran...

Happy 50th Birthday
Amy!
April 20, 1959
"Like a Fine Wine...."
All our Love, Sean, Ben, and Steph

Mrs. Ella Bl...
Ella B. Wel...
April 11, 2...
who's 80!
Family joins to celebrate Blassingame Web... birthday on Sunday...

I have forgotten about the talent show and panic, suddenly remembering that I am good at nothing.

Trudy says she wishes we could all live here together. The cumulative effect of so much pain is to create a space where it feels normal to ache.

~

One night the director brings an old Super-8 he bought at a garage sale, and I try my hand at film. After learning the basics, I decide to make a documentary and spend a week collecting footage of the others as they seek out their moments of happiness. I find that when I'm behind the camera, Vanessa lets me get closer than usual. I follow as she goes about the evening. She will not meet the camera's eye, but the quality of her movements suggests a keen awareness of its bead upon her.

I'm filming Trudy with her trumpet, take after take, to capture an elaborate run of sixteenth notes. "I want there to be evidence," she says, "that I got it right at least once."

When she finally succeeds, Trudy throws her arms around me. It feels surprisingly good to touch someone.

Our embrace is interrupted by a jarring sound. At the far end of the room, Vanessa, hammer in hand, is pounding on a slab of marble.

"What is it that you see in her?" asks Trudy.

"She's making all this possible," I say.

Trudy considers this, weighing whether it's worth her breath to argue. "I think you're barking up the wrong tree," she tells me.

"I haven't had a drink in seven weeks," I say.

She touches my face. "I'd be so good for you," she says.

"And I'd be terrible for you," I say. "Keep practicing your trumpet."

~

Most of us agree that the director's plan is working. We're thriving with our surrogate obsessions. In building dams against our worst compulsions, we've each begun anew.

All except Vanessa, who seems too practiced in the seductive arts to be thought of as an amateur. She knows so well what she is up to that the men in the workshop, fresh from the chrysalis, don't stand a fighting chance.

While Irwin perfects his recipes and Trudy practices her scales, Vanessa has established a regular conquest of one man per week. The cycle is so predictable that I have marked on my calendar the exact night when she will

finally be mine. It's as if I know the date and time of my own demise. If Vanessa is the apple, I'm waiting in a temporary paradise. I will tumble someday, backward from this ladder I am balancing upon.

~

On my machine, Marco's latest message: a litany of outrage followed by jagged, broken laughter.

It triggers recall—shattered windows, orange wallpaper, the scent of ammonia. I don't know if it's dream or memory. I've lost my sense of how to tell the difference.

~

There is a basket of old magazines to use for collage. With scissors and glue, I explore themes of abandonment and neglect, inventing a childhood that might justify my lost decade. I select domestic icons and invert them. I cut bold, angry words from headlines and paste them in a border around the page. My completed work is hung on the wall, and we discuss it in a group. The consensus is that I have miles to go, but that I'm making progress. I look to Vanessa for her take, but she has wandered off with Marcel. In the quiet that follows, I can hear the faint whir of the band saw down the hall.

The open house. The children come. We've hired a clown to entertain them. There are games and contests and prizes. There is punch and several kinds of cookies. The director hands out name tags and shakes hands. I keep to the periphery, observing the proceedings through the camera lens. Everyone is well behaved, forgiving, patient, and inspired. It feels like the days leading up to Christmas. Vanessa wears a long black dress. I've never seen her look so beautiful.

Vanessa's ex-husband is there with their daughter. I feel no jealousy as I watch them interact. They do not seem to know one another. At the end of the night, there is an argument. Vanessa shouts and the man and child leave, the little girl in tears.

~

Marco calls every fifteen minutes and talks until the machine cuts him off. He is with a girl who laughs and calls me by name. She has a familiar voice. I lie in bed, trying to place it. Throughout the night, a narrative evolves in 30-second fragments. They are heading somewhere, getting closer to something. Or so I imagine. They are drunk and on another planet.

At four in the morning, I take the phone off the hook. The next day I change the number.

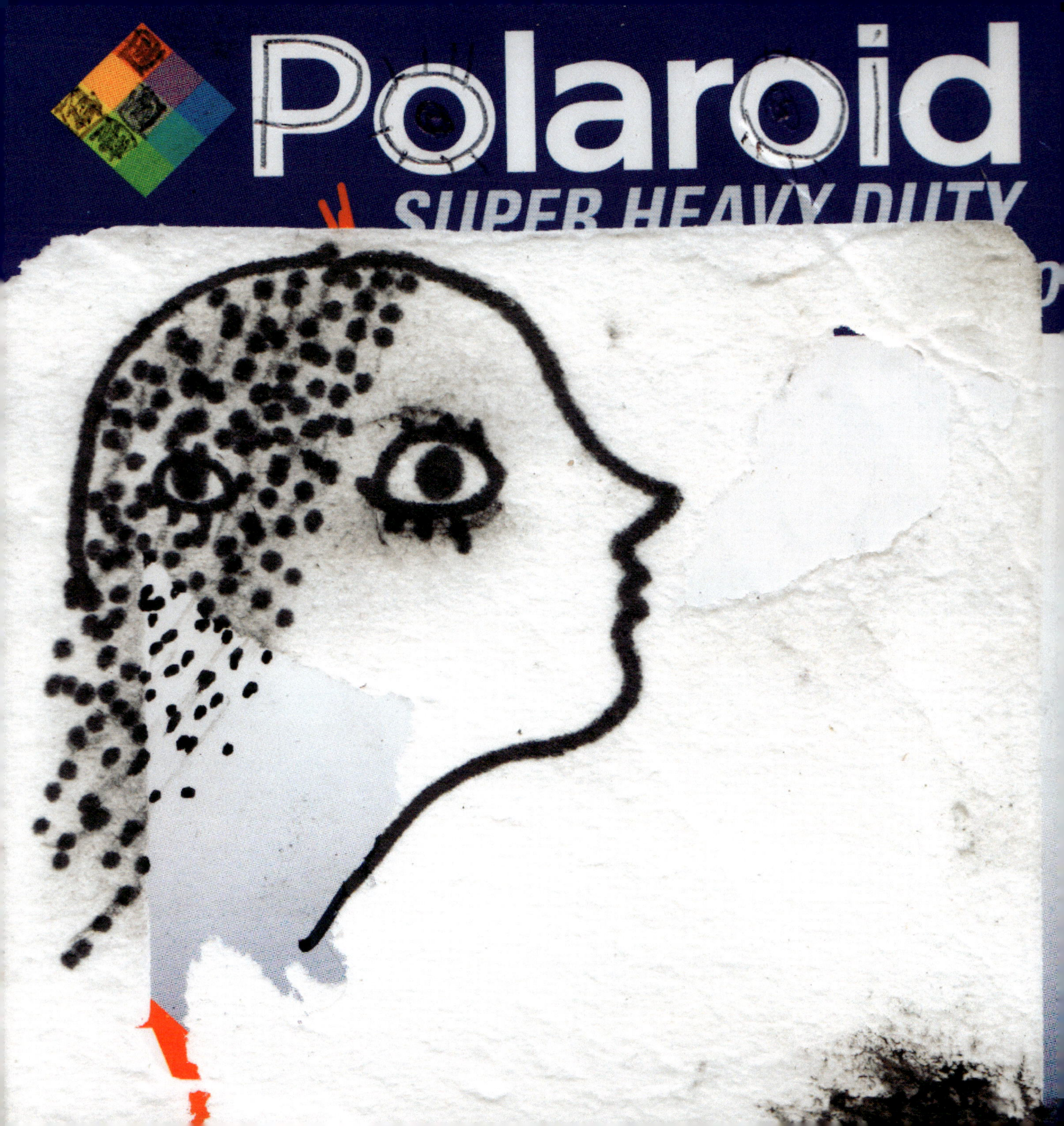
Polaroid
SUPER HEAVY DUTY

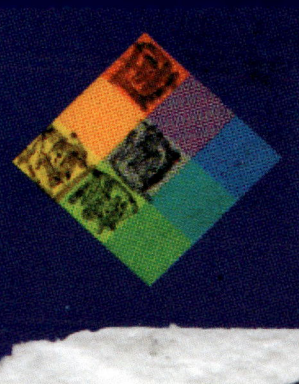

Jackie is the first of us to miss a meeting. We call her at home, but the machine picks up. Irwin swears he can smell vodka right through the receiver.

We sit in a circle and hold hands. We assure ourselves that we are not like Jackie. She is not a bad person, we say, but she was not yet ready for this step. We intend to give each other strength, but instead we gossip in our jealousy and discover that superiority is a weak placebo.

"I have an idea," says Eddie, who was a wrestler in college.

We gather all of the pillows and blankets we can find to cushion the floor of the multipurpose room and take turns body-slamming one another. The sensation is so familiar. We try to remind ourselves of the bad parts, because all that comes to mind when we think of the past is the sweet spurned lover with outstretched arms, so willing to receive us and forgive.

~

I have moved through the visual media and have not found my niche. Today I begin a series of poems. I have always enjoyed the texture and rhythm of words. But the blank white paper is terrifying, and Freddie suggests I try heroic couplets. The structure, he says,

might help me find my way. Freddie has just begun his second novel of the week. His typewriter sounds like an automatic weapon.

~

Recollections in waves: quilt blocks of light and dark sliding in and out of focus. Explanations emerge from the haze. Names come to mind with a jarring clarity. Voices taunt. Stories unfold, the people I admired suddenly turning out to be bad guys after all.

I want to ignore it or suppress it, but I can't. Or I won't. It's too interesting. This is my life, and it's finally, actually interesting.

~

The talent show. Laura in a box as Scott saws her in half. The two halves separate. Laura's feet continue to wiggle. The illusion is satisfying.

Mona sings Happy Birthday with her version of a sexy drawl. She wraps her scarf around my neck and wriggles in my lap. I have no idea how she knew, but I am touched.

Herman sits quietly and still for a full sixty seconds, a thing he's been able to manage only recently. We clap and sing his praises. We say we understand.

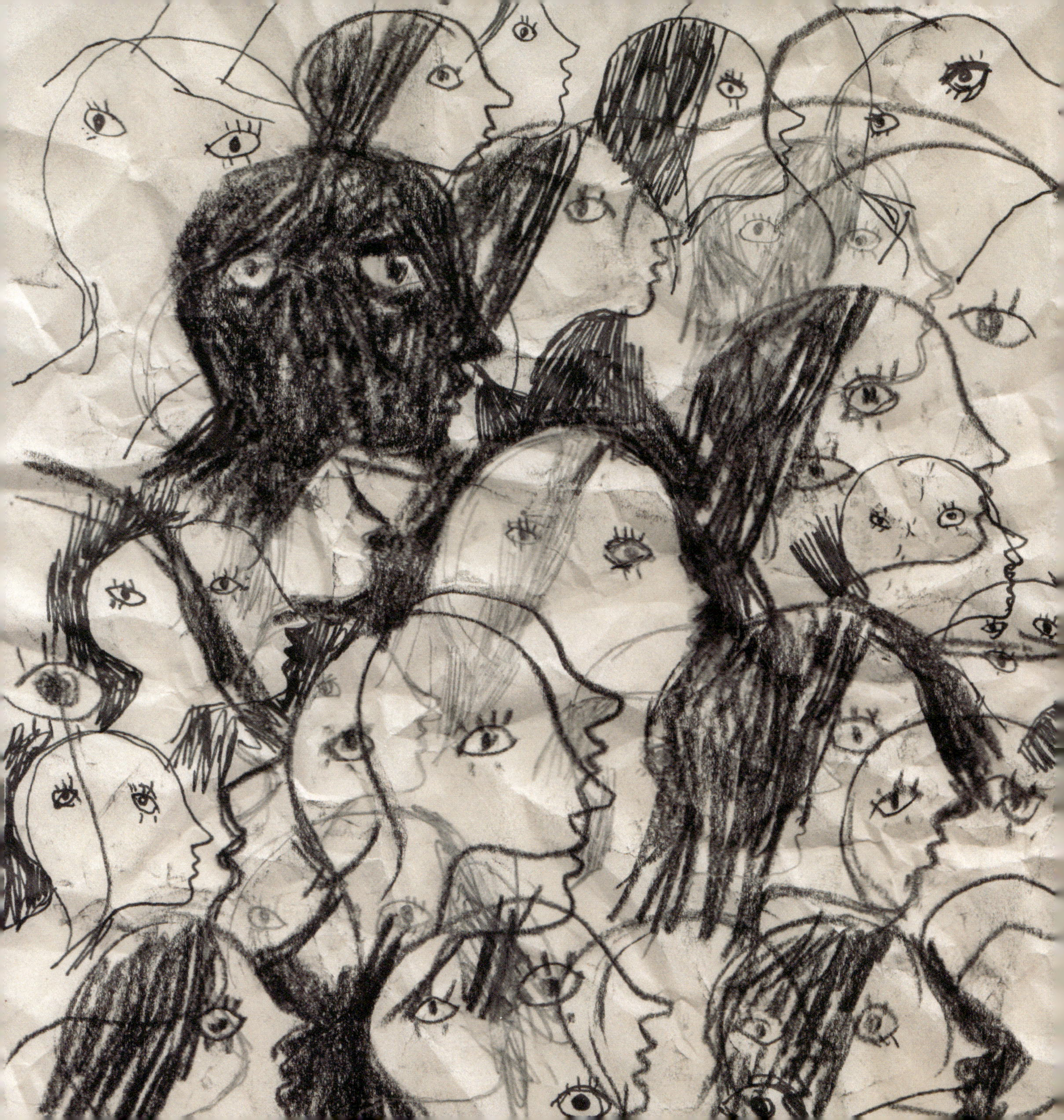

Vanessa, in a black cape, will suck the blood from the neck of a male volunteer. No one raises his hand. Vanessa stomps her foot and pouts. Reluctantly, Lenny rises from his chair and goes to the front of the room.

My turn comes. I apologize but allow that I have nothing to share. I have written a poem for Vanessa, but I cannot bring myself to read it. The others are angry. I have broken the covenant. After seeing them naked, I have hidden in my modesty.

Later, after the director has gone, Vanessa and all the men but me engage in a spirited orgy on the shag carpet in the sewing room. The sound is extraordinary, regular and mechanical like the thrum of the Berninas. When the other women join in eventually, I set up my camera and start to film.

Trudy waves, beckoning. It seems I am forgiven. I smile and wave back, grateful but declining. I am content to stand here for their sakes. I have learned in weeks of watching that this only works if we can believe that it works. And that in order to believe, someone must be there to affirm what we think we might be feeling. To make these tenuous versions of happiness real, someone has to stand on the far side of the room, back against the door, witness and apostle, taking it all in.

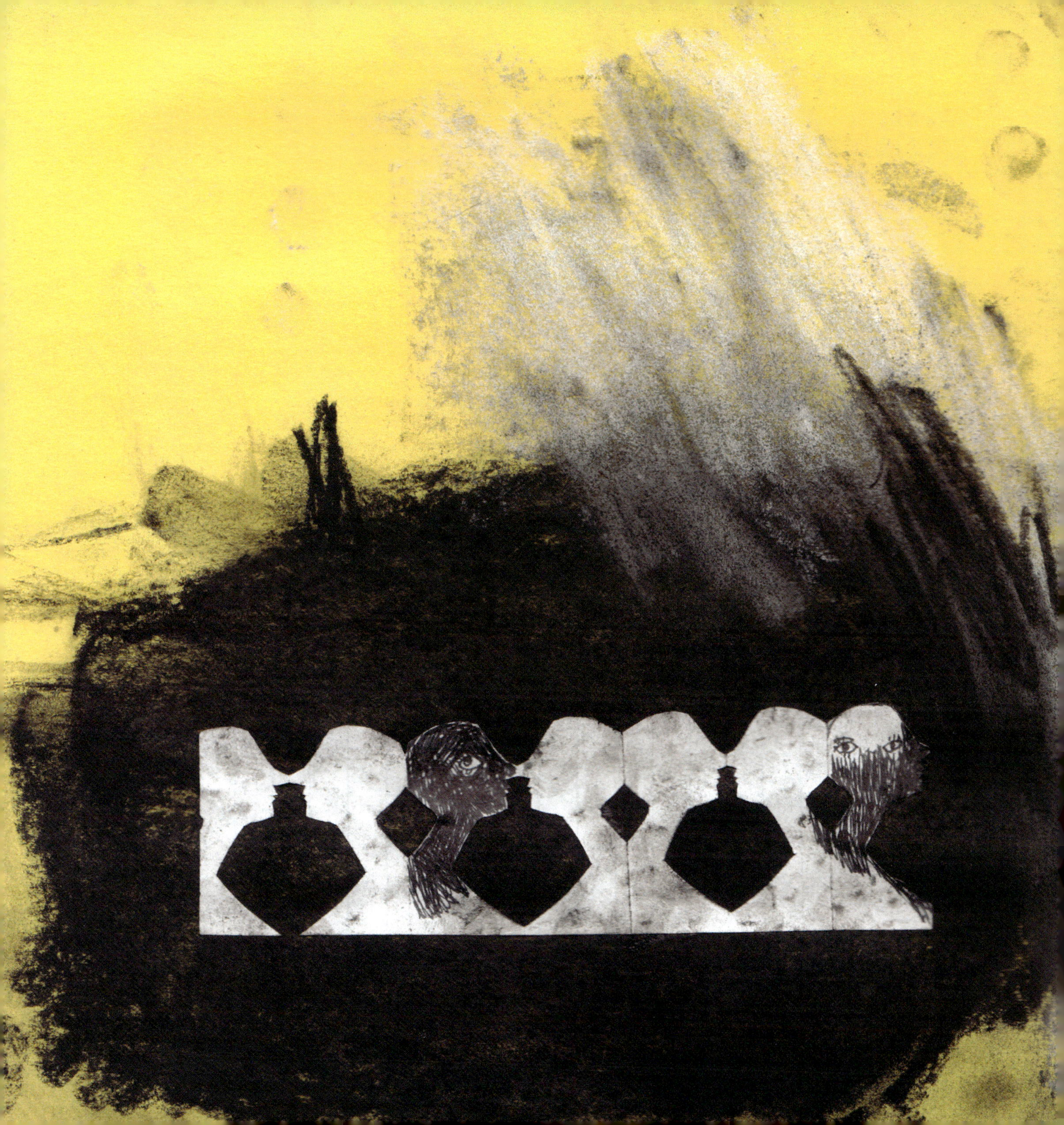

Workshop has ended for the night. I have stayed late to finish editing my film. Vanessa stands in the doorway. She speaks my name. In spite of my anticipation, I do not look up from my work. I have known that she would find me, that she will not leave without taking what she's come for. There is nowhere else for her to go. It is the thirteenth week. I am the last man standing.

Deleted moments of our lives lie like noodles at my feet. "I'm steering the footage in a new direction," I tell her. "The first ending was far too dark."

Vanessa is trembling. "Kiss me," she says.

I push her away. She looks at me like she's been slapped.

"Isn't this what you wanted?" she asks.

I take Vanessa's hand and lead her to a chair. "Wait," I tell her. "I have to show you something first."

I load the reel and turn on the projector. I point to the screen. Vanessa resists, but starts to focus as the film begins.

Jackie is laughing. It is footage from her last night in workshop. There is no sign of the doubts that she must have been feeling. She is dancing with Freddie. She is light and free as he swings and then lifts her.

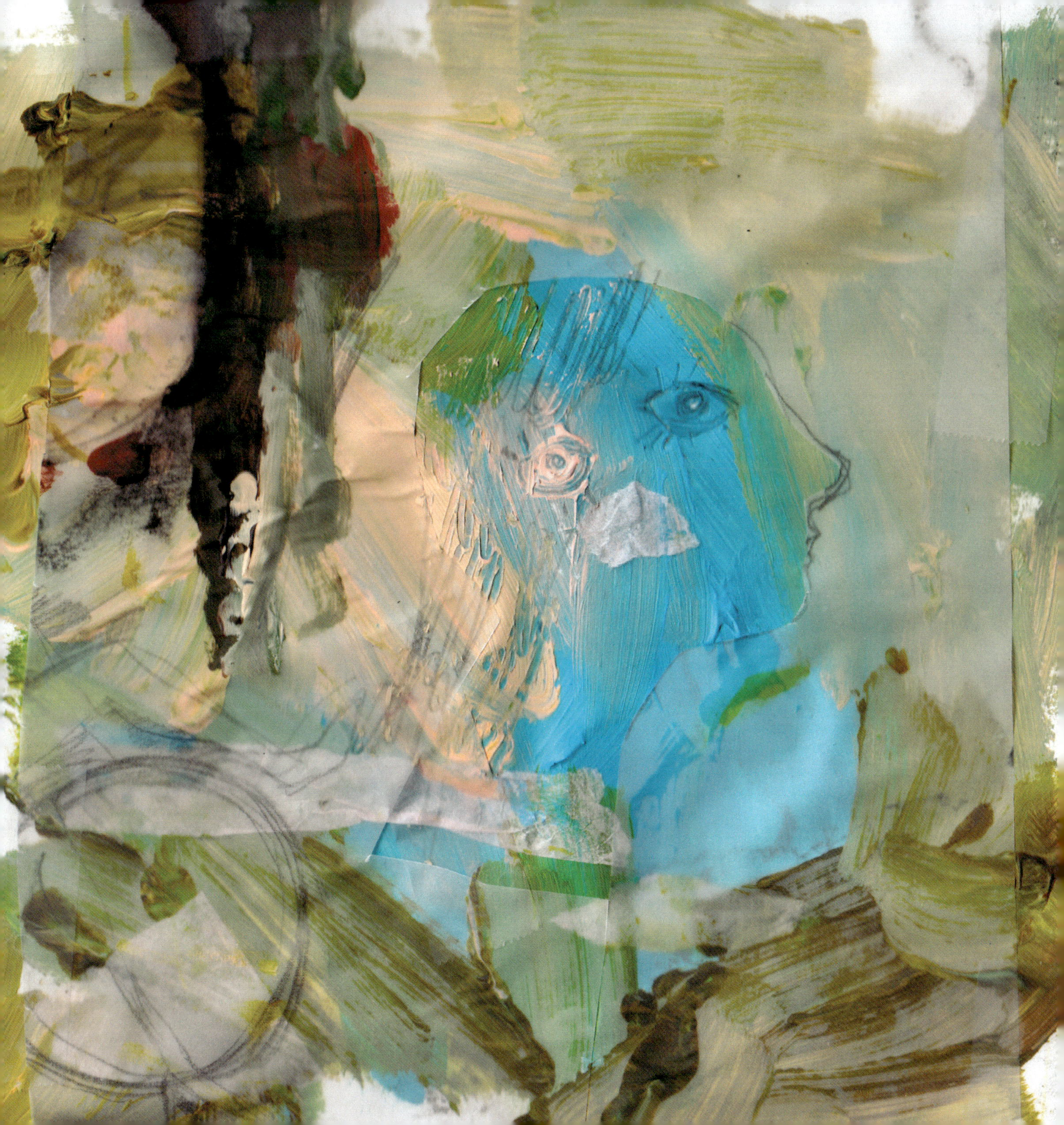

Then: Irwin smiling over the perfect cappuccino—pristine foam with a scattering of nutmeg and a bright green sprig of mint. Daphne sips deeply and is satisfied. Irwin is so happy.

Vanessa watches. The projector flickers. Trudy plays a flawless reveille and lifts her trumpet skyward with a flourish at the end.

Michael at the lathe, turning a lamp stand. "For my mom," he tells the camera. "I've never made her things before."

Vanessa with her daughter on the evening of the open house, blank and uncertain as if greeting a stranger. The little girl, clutching her father's hand, is shy. The man looks kind. He wants to be here. They stand there for a while, everyone so patient.

The camera moves in: Vanessa inhales deliberately. It's taking all her concentration to keep on breathing. The camera, suspended, floats without judgment. We still don't know which way this is going to go—the man, the girl, Vanessa in a standoff. No one blinks.

The moment passes and Vanessa crumbles. She smiles through the tears and touches her lips to the little girl's forehead. She takes her daughter by the hand, a finger in a fist, leads her to the meeting room, and shows her some drawings she's made of rainbows.

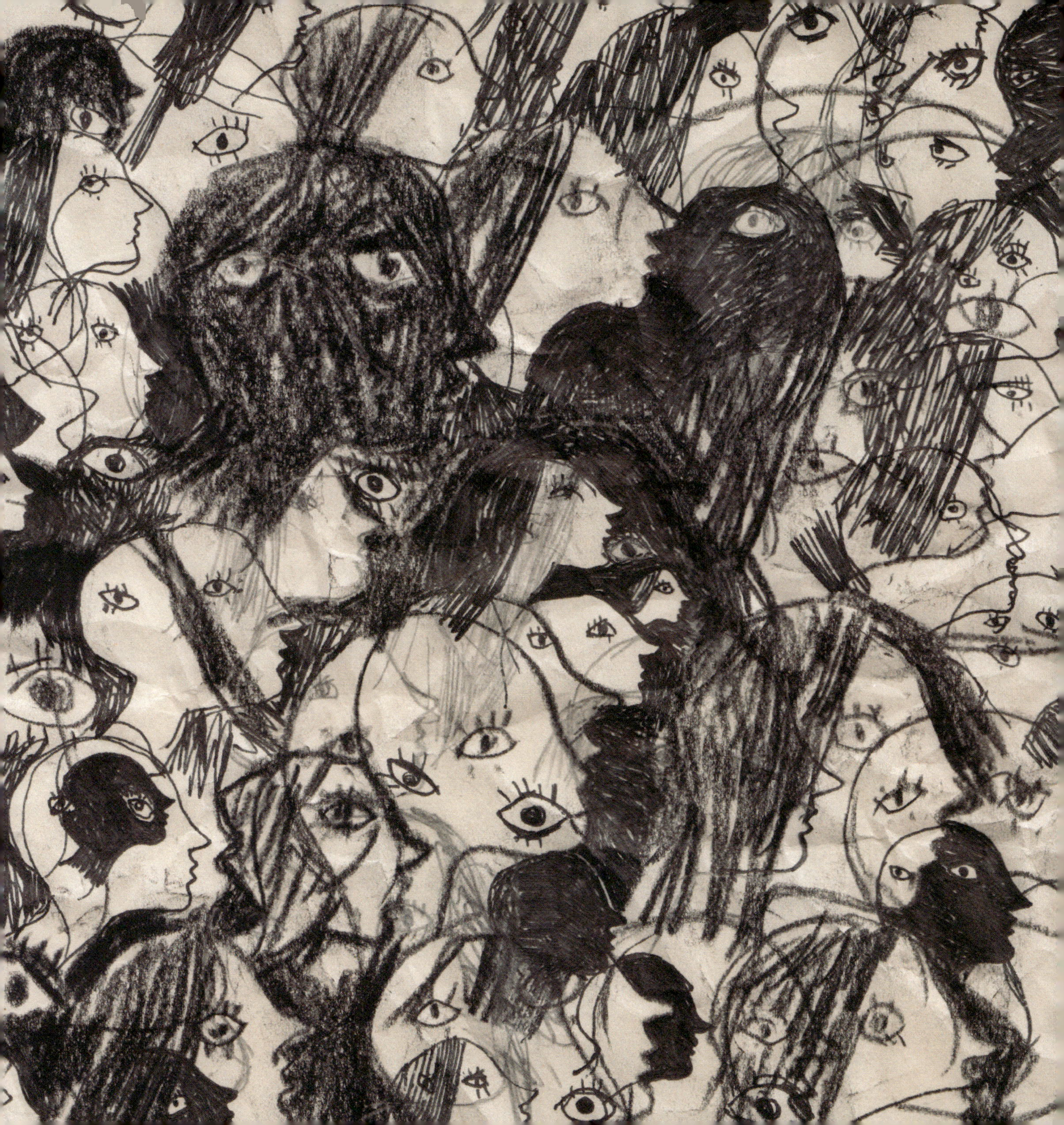

The film ends. I turn off the projector. Vanessa turns toward me but averts her eyes. "Thank you," she says, "for not showing the rest."

"That's all there is," I say.

She nods and tries to smile. She turns toward the screen. "Play it again?" she asks.

I rethread the film and we watch a second time.

"She's so happy," Vanessa says, when Trudy's face appears.

~

"It's your turn," Vanessa tells me, when the movie ends again. "I've saved the best for last." She grabs at my buttons, pulling me toward her. As we embrace, the reality of flesh distorts my understanding of a woman I've known in every other medium. I am surprised to discover that her body is warm, that her hair smells like shampoo, that her arms have weight.

Vanessa and I have just begun the next part of our long and aching lives. Even by the best scenario, we will spend hereafter in a state of stinging incompleteness. We're in the final scene of the first act. There will be dialogue and crisis, and when the lights come down, only one of us can still be standing on the stage.

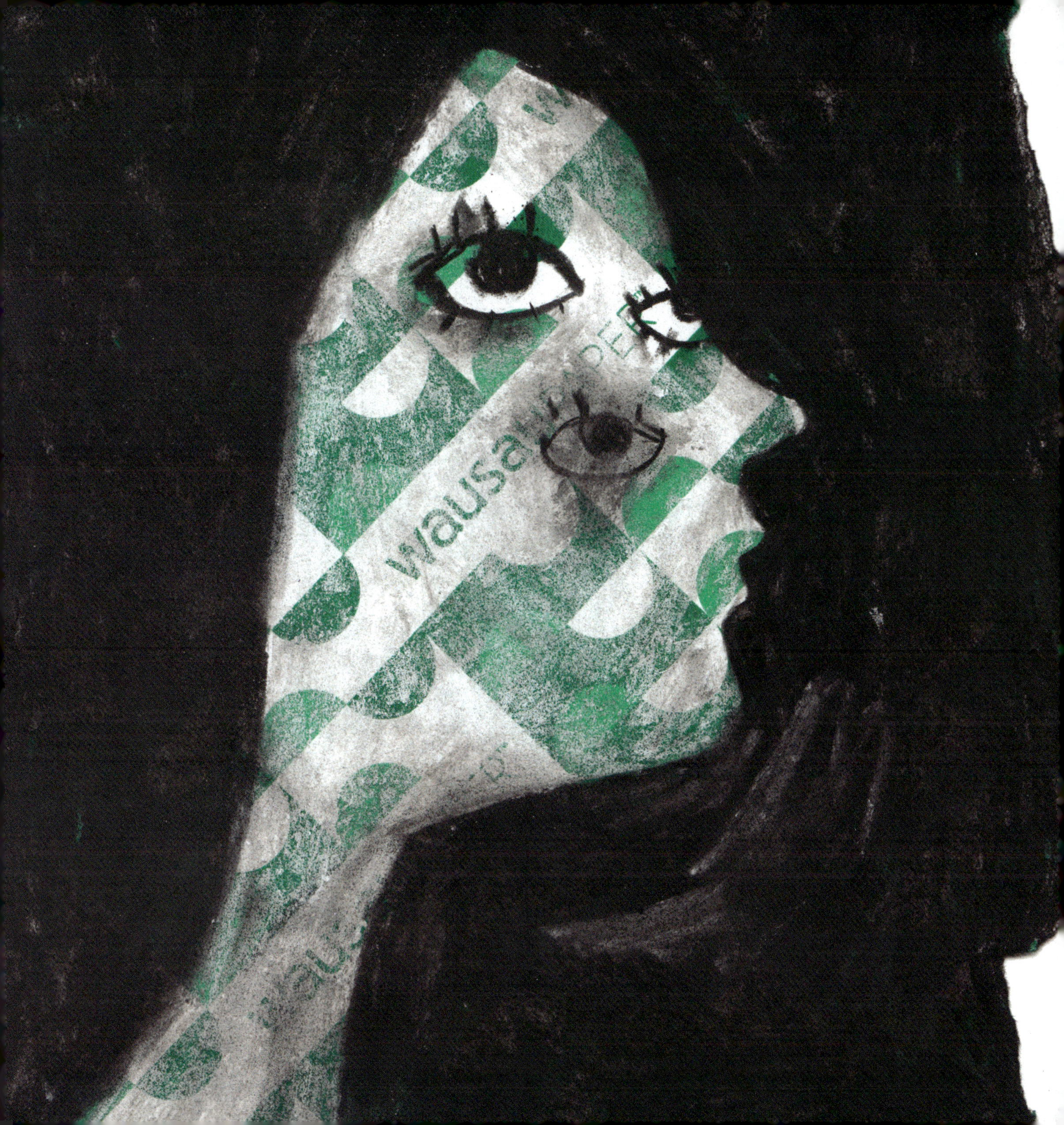
wausau

Or neither of us might, it occurs to me.

Vanessa waits, lips parted, arms around me. Her dress is thin. It's getting late. We are all that's left.

I push her away.

"I need this," she says.

"Let's watch the movie one more time," I say.

"And then?" she asks.

"Of course," I say.

Relieved, Vanessa smiles at me, and I can hardly recognize her.

~

When Jackie's face appears on the screen, I walk out of the room. Vanessa, transfixed, doesn't notice. Since her new life began, I have always been there. In her mind, I always will. I wait in the hallway until the film runs out and I can hear it clicking on the spool. I picture her face as she notices I'm gone. I close my eyes and savor the way the air breaks when my name escapes her lips—her voice, confused at first, then angry, then leavening into despair.

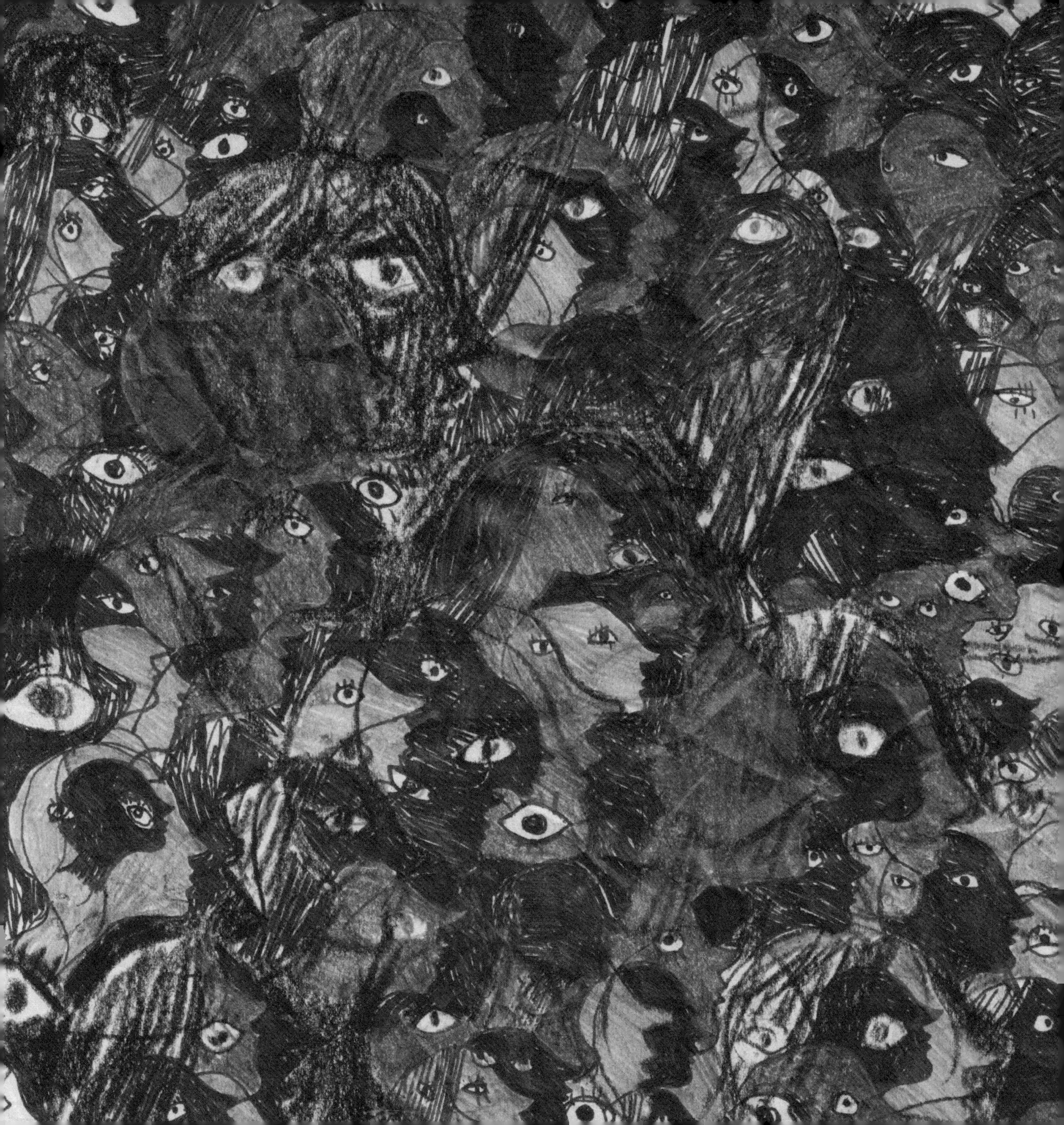

I turn and walk down the hall. When I hear her behind me, I break into a run, just slow enough that she can keep pace. It's my turn now. I will lead Vanessa for a while, ever at an arm's length, for both of our sakes.

I push through the double doors and out into the night. It's cold and clear and I can see my breath. I wait a moment on the sidewalk. When Vanessa opens the door, I keep on running.

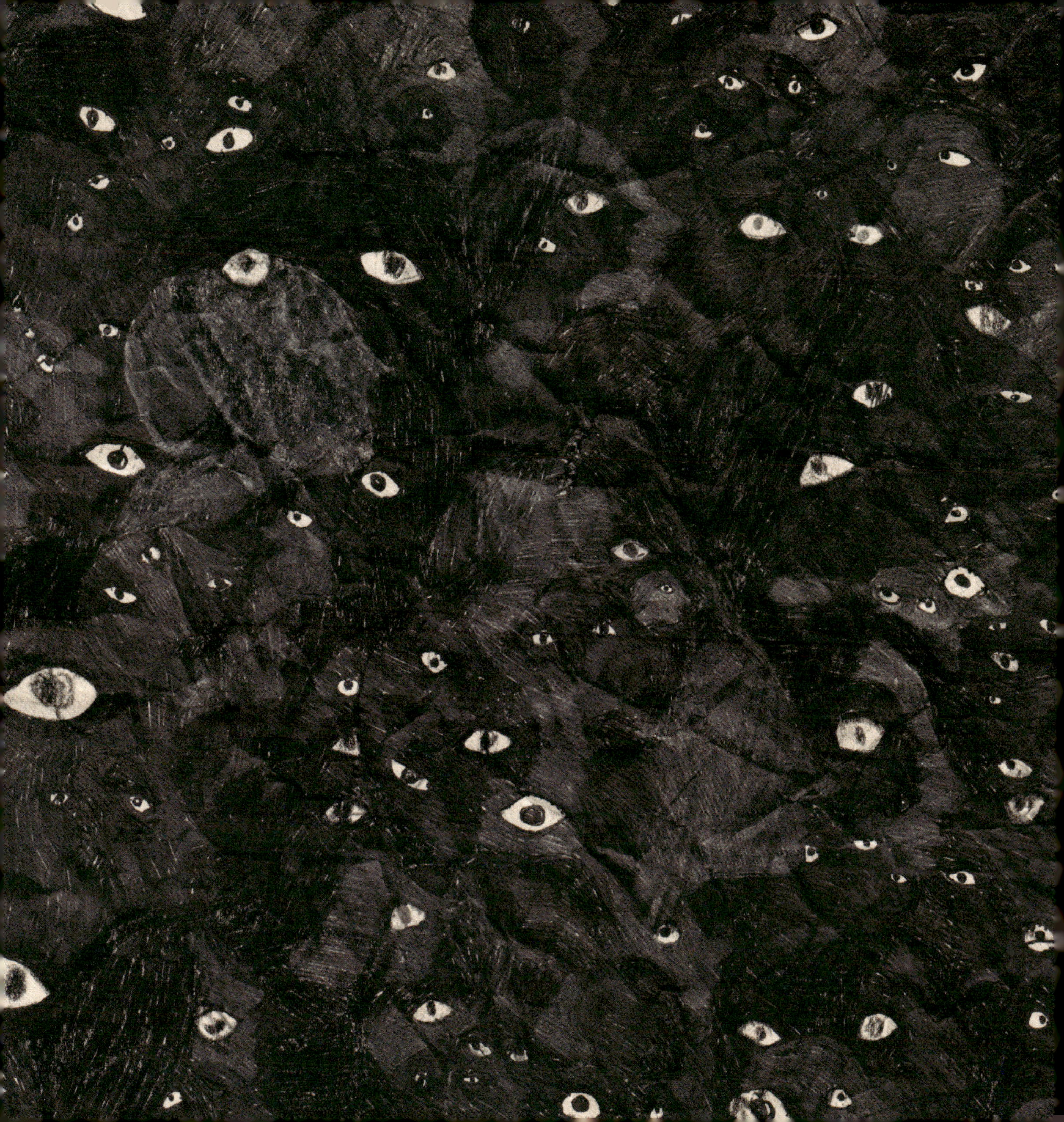

This Idiots'Books creation is the product of collaboration between Matthew Swanson and Robbi Behr. The current title attempts to rectify what some detractors have observed as a disturbing paucity of black ink in past volumes.

Matthew is a writer/harmonica player/person who wishes he could draw but can't, yet sometimes tries to anyway, much to the amusement of Robbi, who laughs and points and heckles, causing Matthew to feel a rare brand of shame that is almost, but not quite, painful enough to keep him from trying to draw yet again.

Robbi is an illustrator/commercial salmon fisherwoman/person who wishes she could write and can, and who lords it over Matthew at every opportunity. She recently produced a son, who appeared precisely 33 minutes after she arrived at the hospital, proving from the start that he does not share his mother's tendency to be late to everything.

They live in the hayloft of a barn in Chestertown, Maryland.

Also by Idiots' Books

Facial Features of French Explorers (Vol. 1)
Death of Henry (Vol. 2)
Ten Thousand Stories (Vol. 3)
Man Joe Rises (Vol. 4)
Unattractive and Inadequate (Vol. 5)
Richard Nixon (Vol. 6)
Understanding Traffic (Vol. 7)
Dawn of the Fats (Vol. 8)
The Contented (Vol. 9)
The Clearing (Vol. 10)
George Washington Slept Here (Vol. 11)
Last Day (Vol. 12)
The Nearly Perfect Sisters of the Holy Bliss (Vol. 13)
The Vast Sahara (Vol. 14)
The Baby is Disappointing (Vol. 15)

Let Me Count the Ways (Vol. 16)
Animal House (Vol. 17)
After Everafter (Vol. 18)
Floating on the Ocean (Vol. 19)
Jericho (Vol. 20)
The Last of the Real Small Farmers (Vol. 21)
Tarpits and Canyonlands (Vol. 22)
Nasty Chipmunk (Vol. 23)
The New South (Vol. 24)

For the Love of God
A Bully Named Chuck
My Henderson Robot
St. Michaels: The Town That Somehow Fooled the British

Yearly subscriptions (6 Volumes) to Idiots' Books are available for $60.
Go to www.idiotsbooks.com to subscribe. Right now.

From the Inside Out
Copyright © February 2010
Idiots' Books Vol. 25
www.idiotsbooks.com

See also:
www.robbibehr.com